My Spring Robin

By Anne Rockwell
Pictures by Harlow Rockwell & Lizzy Rockwell

MACMILLAN PUBLISHING COMPANY · NEW YORK

COLLIER MACMILLAN PUBLISHERS · LONDON

For Dr. Mike Marino

Text copyright © 1989 by Anne Rockwell
Illustrations copyright © 1989 by Harlow Rockwell and Lizzy Rockwell
Macmillan Publishing Company
866 Third Avenue, New York, NY 10022
Collier Macmillan Canada, Inc.
Printed and bound in Japan
First American Edition
10 9 8 7 6 5 4 3 2 1
The text of this book is set in 24 point Spartan Book.
The illustrations are rendered in pencil and watercolor.
Library of Congress Cataloging-in-Publication Data
Rockwell, Anne F. My spring robin/by Anne Rockwell; pictures by
Harlow Rockwell and Lizzy Rockwell.—1st ed.   p.   cm.
Summary: Before finding the robin she is searching for, a child
discovers other interesting fauna and flora in her backyard.
ISBN 0-02-777611-5
[1. Spring—Fiction. 2. Robins—Fiction. 3. Nature—Fiction.]
I. Rockwell, Harlow, ill. II. Rockwell, Lizzy, ill. III. Title.
PZ7.R5943Mym 1989   [E]—dc19   88-13333 CIP AC

A robin sang a song for me
every day last summer.
I liked that robin.

But in the fall
my robin flew away.
My father said
it would come back
in the spring.
So when spring came,

I went looking for my spring robin.

I saw a bee
taking honey from a crocus,
but I didn't see my robin.

I looked into the yellow forsythia bush,

but my robin wasn't there.

My robin was not sitting
high up in the branches
of the magnolia tree.

In the fern garden
behind our outdoor table,

fuzzy fiddleheads were sprouting
in last year's wet, brown leaves.

But I didn't see
my robin there.

I saw a tiny toad.
It hopped behind
a clump of daffodils
to hide from me.

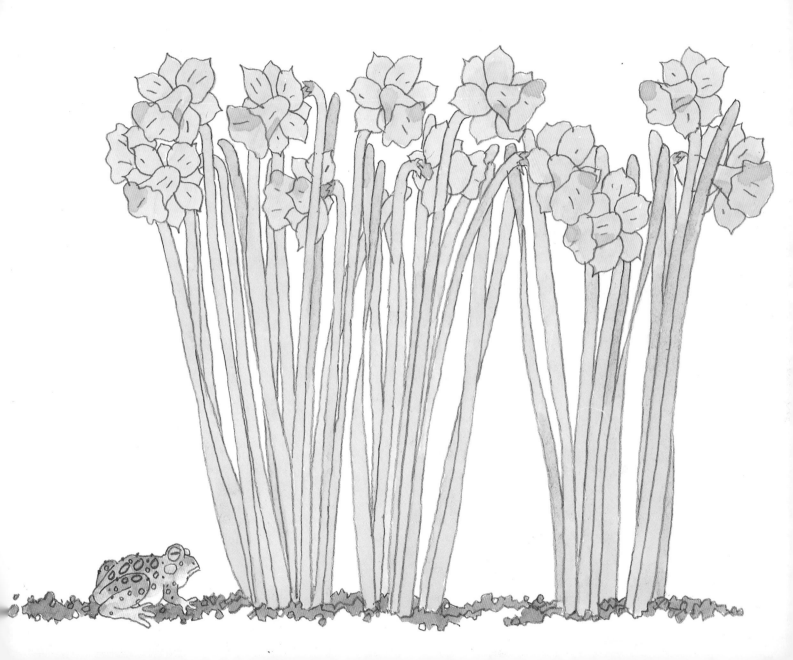

I looked high up into the sky
to see if my robin
was flying back to me.
Drops of rain fell on my face,
and our neighbor's cat ran home.

After the shower I picked
a little bunch of purple violets
for my mother.
I watched a shiny earthworm
wriggle up out of the ground.

And then I heard it.
I heard that song!
"Cheer-up, cheerilee!
Cheer-up, cheerilee!
Cheer-up, cheerilee!"
I knew who was singing that song!

It was my spring robin!